THE BOXCAR CHILDREN MYSTERIES

THE BOXCAR CHILDREN

CREATED BY
GERTRUDE CHANDLER WARNER

BOOK

155

THE MYSTERY OF THE FORGOTTEN FAMILY

ILLUSTRATED BY
ANTHONY VanARSDALE

ALBERT WHITMAN & COMPANY
CHICAGO, ILLINOIS

ISBN 978-0-8075-0768-1 (hardcover)
ISBN 978-0-8075-0769-8 (paperback)
ISBN 978-0-8075-0770-4 (ebook)

Printed in the United States of America
10 9 8 7 6 5 4 3 2 1 LB 24 23 22 21 20 19

Illustrations by Anthony VanArsdale

Visit the Boxcar Children online at www.boxcarchildren.com.
For more information about Albert Whitman & Company,
visit our website at www.albertwhitman.com.

Contents

CHAPTER 1

Past Forgotten

The bright summer sun shone warmly on the four Alden children. Henry, Jessie, Violet, and Benny stood in front of an antique shop on Main Street, looking at a sign on the door.

"'Come...in...'" Benny said slowly. He was six and still learning to read. "'Mul...Muldaur's Shop has re...re...'"

"'Reopened for business,'" said ten-year-old Violet, finishing the sentence.

Benny squinted at the sign. "Reopened? Do you think that means somebody else is here instead of Mr. Muldaur?"

The Aldens had been to Muldaur's Antique Shop

a few times, and each time, the shop's owner, Mr. Muldaur, had been in a bad mood. The last time the children had visited, Mr. Muldaur had gotten upset at Benny for petting the dog that often hung out in the shop.

"Look here," said Violet. She pointed to some small writing on the bottom of the sign: "'Muldaur's Antique Shop was closed last week due to illness. We apologize for any problems this has caused our customers.'"

"It sounds like Mr. Muldaur was out sick," Jessie said. "I'm sure he's back now."

Benny frowned. Although he did not want Mr. Muldaur to be sick, he did not want to be yelled at again either. "I think I'll stay out here and watch our bikes," Benny said.

Henry and Jessie gave each other a look. They knew why Benny did not want to go inside. But they couldn't leave Benny on his own. At fourteen and twelve, Henry and Jessie knew just what would change Benny's mind.

"Suit yourself, Benny," Jessie said. "That will leave more toys for me to find."

Benny looked up. "Toys?"

Henry nodded. "That's right. And hidden treasures for me. Who knows what kinds of things we can find to put in the boxcar."

Henry opened the door to the shop, and little bells jingled on the doorframe. Slowly, Henry, Jessie, and Violet made their way into the shop.

A moment later the door jingled again, and Benny came inside. "It's too hot outside," he said. Then he whispered, "Do you really think we'll find treasure for the boxcar?"

The Alden children loved the old boxcar that sat in their backyard. For a little while, it had been their home. After the children's parents had died, they'd run away. They had been worried their grandfather would be mean. The children found the boxcar in the forest and used it for shelter. The children had all sorts of adventures in the boxcar. They even found their dog, Watch!

After a while, Grandfather had found them. He wasn't mean at all! Grandfather brought the children to live in his big house, and he even brought the boxcar to be the children's clubhouse.

Jessie smiled at her little brother. "First we need to find Mrs. McGregor's gift," she said.

Mrs. McGregor was the Aldens' housekeeper. She was like family to the children, and her birthday was coming up. The children wanted to get her something special.

"I think it will be near the glassware," said Violet. Mrs. McGregor loved collecting antiques. She had a whole set of matching serving pieces. The only piece she was missing was a salt server, and Violet had found the perfect one on the Muldaur Antiques website.

"What is a salt server anyway?" said Benny.

"It's a little bowl you put salt into when you serve a fancy dinner," said Violet. "It comes with a tiny spoon too."

Benny thought that sounded boring. But he was excited to look at all of the items in the crowded shop. The room was filled with shelves and shelves of old objects, large and small. There were lamps, books, toys, jewelry, framed pictures, and clocks. There were birdcages, musical instruments, dolls, hats, and umbrellas. There seemed to be too many things to name or count.

Violet found shelves with silver plates and other serving pieces. "I think I see it!" she said. She walked over and took down a small bowl with a lid. A tiny silver spoon was nestled inside. "Mrs. McGregor's salt server!" said Violet. "I'm glad it's still here."

"Great," said Henry, taking out his wallet. "Though I don't see anyone to pay."

"Hello?" a voice called from the back of the shop. "Is someone here?"

A tall man with curly black hair came down the aisle where the Aldens were standing. Benny hid behind his older brother. He thought for sure Mr. Muldaur was going to yell at them for something.

But the shop owner spoke in a cheery voice. "Ah, there you are! What can I do for you children today?"

"Good morning, Mr. Muldaur," said Henry. "Are you feeling all right? We saw on the sign that you were sick."

Mr. Muldaur put his hand up to a white bandage wrapped around his head. "Yes, I had a bit of an accident, but I'm doing better now. Today is my

first day back—just trying to get things sorted out."

A big golden retriever trotted over to the children, wagging her tail.

"Mitzy!" said Violet. She bent down. Then she stopped. "Can we pet her, Mr. Muldaur?"

"Of course you may!" said Mr. Muldaur. Then a confused look came across his face. "But how do you know her name? Do I know you children?"

For a moment, no one spoke. "We're the Aldens, Mr. Muldaur," Henry said finally. "You know us, and we know you and Mitzy too. We've been in your store a few times."

Mr. Muldaur sighed. "Is that so?" For the first time, his smile faded. "I'm afraid I've forgotten quite a bit since the accident."

"What happened?" asked Violet.

Mr. Muldaur sat down in an old rocking chair. Then he continued: "I only remember one thing from that day last week. I was climbing up my ladder to get something on a high shelf." The man shook his head. "I must have fallen because I woke up in the hospital the next morning with a terrible headache. The doctors kept me there for three days."

"That's horrible!" said Jessie. "How did they find you?"

Mr. Muldaur reached down to pet Mitzy. "My wonderful dog saved me," he said. "I was unconscious, and Mitzy barked and barked until someone came. What a good girl, Mitzy!"

The children had never seen Mr. Muldaur so happy before. "You seem...different," said Henry. "Are you sure you're ready to come back to work?"

"I feel great!" said Mr. Muldaur. "It's just my memory...The doctors told me it would return, but they don't know how long it will take. I can't seem to make much sense out of anything in my store."

"You did know an awful lot about your antiques," said Jessie. She thought back to the times they had visited the shop. It always seemed like Mr. Muldaur had a story for every little thing.

Mr. Muldaur smiled as he looked all around his shop. "And I remember that it's my job to know about all these things," he said. "That's what people in the antique business do. We learn about each item so we can tell customers where, when, and how it was made. We try to learn about the journey each item has taken, from its being made all the way to this store."

"Do you remember any stories about this?" asked Violet. She held out the salt server.

Mr. Muldaur sighed and shook his head. "I'm sorry, I don't. But maybe I'll have a story soon," he said.

Benny had found the toy area and came back with an old mechanical windup bear. "What do you mean about journeys? Did this bear march here?"

Mr. Muldaur chuckled. "That would be a very interesting journey indeed!" Mr. Muldaur took the bear in his hands. "I am talking about a different kind of journey. This might have been passed down from one family member to another over many years. Or it might have gone from child to child, crossing the country, maybe even the world! I'm sure this bear has had a very interesting journey... It's part of what makes it special."

Mr. Muldaur turned the bear on its side. He

began winding it up with the key that stuck out from the side.

"Could this bear be really old then?" asked Benny. "Like, even older than Grandfather?"

Mr. Muldaur laughed. "Yes, it may be, though I don't remember your grandfather, or any stories about the bear anymore." He set the bear down on a table, where it slowly walked along on all fours, moving its head from side to side. Benny laughed as he watched the bear lumber ahead.

"Well, you do know our grandfather," said Violet. "Maybe when you meet him, you'll remember him."

"I sure hope so," said Mr. Muldaur. "And I hope my memory hurries up and comes back. If not, I won't be very helpful in selling these wonderful antiques."

The Alden children looked at one another. When they had first come into the shop, they had wanted to get in and out as quickly as possible. But they could tell Mr. Muldaur needed help. Jessie and Henry nodded at each other.

"Maybe we can help you get organized," said Jessie. "Until your memory comes back."

Mr. Muldaur was surprised. "Are you sure?" he asked.

"Yes!" said Benny. "We're good at finding out secrets!" The thought of hidden treasures and old secrets made him forget all about the last time he had visited the shop.

"All right, come with me," said Mr. Muldaur, standing up. "Into my 'secret office.'"

He led the children behind a bookcase in the back of the shop. There was small room with a huge wooden desk, which was buried under an equally huge pile of papers. There were more stacks of paper scattered on shelves. Open filing cabinets stood against the walls, stuffed with even more loose paper.

"It isn't really a secret office," said Mr. Muldaur. "It's more of a secret pile of paper." He chuckled. "I'm sure I wrote everything down. But I have no idea which papers belong to which items. Everything is all jumbled up. Sort of how my mind feels these days."

Mr. Muldaur looked up with a glint in his eye. "Still," he said, "I'm happy to feel better and to be back with my shop and my dog. And I've met you four! This must be my lucky day."

"You're meeting us again!" said Benny. "And it's double lucky. We're on summer vacation. We can help you a lot."

CHAPTER 2

Curious Customers

"Right now, I've got some errands to run," said Mr. Muldaur. "Since the accident, I haven't had anyone around to be able to keep an eye on things. Would you children be able to watch the shop and keep Mitzy company while I step out?"

"Of course," said Henry. "We can start organizing too."

"Wonderful," said Mr. Muldaur. He looked around the office. "I can tell you that papers for items of little value are probably in those file cabinets. The ones on the shelves would be next, and the papers on the desk are for things that are of great interest."

"What do you mean 'little value'?" asked Benny.

"Are those things worth less money? Are the things in the desk worth lots of money, like treasure?"

"They *might* be worth a lot of money," said Mr. Muldaur. "But value isn't always about money. Some antiques aren't worth much, but their families value them anyway. Others have value because they are unusual."

"Oh," said Benny. "Then maybe my bear isn't exactly a treasure."

"That depends on what you mean by *treasure*," said Mr. Muldaur. "You know, Benny, I might have a special job just for you." Mr. Muldaur opened a drawer in the desk and took out a cardboard box. Inside the box were dozens of small keys.

"These look like the one in my bear," Benny said. "They all have the same shape, but they're different sizes and colors. Are they for winding things up?"

"Yes, they are," said Mr. Muldaur. "They belong to other mechanical toys. I need someone to match up these keys with the toys they belong to. Do you think you could do that, Benny? You would have to find the toys and then try the keys on each one."

"I sure could!" said Benny. He took the box of keys from Mr. Muldaur and stood up straight. Benny liked having a job to do.

"Is there anything special about the antiques behind the front counter?" asked Jessie. "Those look extra special."

"Yes! You have sharp eyes," said Mr. Muldaur. "Those are my most valuable items. And their papers are..." He rubbed his head for a moment. "In the middle desk drawer! And now I really do need to do those errands."

"Don't worry," said Benny. "While you're gone, we'll take extra good care of Mitzy. And Mitzy will guard your treasures!" Benny patted Mitzy, who stood up and wagged her tail.

Mr. Muldaur laughed. "I'm sure you'll do a great job. See you all soon." He went out the front door.

Jessie looked around the office and took a deep breath. "We've got our work cut out for us," she said, picking up a paper from the top of a stack.

Violet peered at the paper Jessie was holding. "It looks as if each item has its own papers with whatever information Mr. Muldaur knew about it."

"The papers don't have *all* the information, Violet," said Jessie. "Remember the stories Mr. Muldaur knew? They're not here. The papers only tell us what the item is, how much it's worth, and some other facts about it. I sure hope Mr. Muldaur's memory comes back. If it doesn't, how will he be able to tell those interesting stories?"

"I want to know about my bear," said Benny. "I just know he has a good story. Maybe he's worth a whole lot of money now! And...maybe there are more amazing things in this shop!" Benny ran out of the office, and Mitzy followed him.

Henry called them. "Benny, don't forget we're here to help Mr. Muldaur."

Benny called back. "Mitzy and I are guarding! We're doing a good job. And looking for toys."

The other three Aldens laughed.

Then Jessie turned to her brother and sister. "Can you believe Mr. Muldaur is even the same person? Before the accident, he didn't like having children in the shop. Now he's letting us watch it for him."

"He wouldn't let us pet Mitzy before either," said Violet.

Henry shrugged. "The accident really seems to have changed him. I'm glad we can help him get back on his feet."

The children turned back to the stack of papers. They started by looking for any sign of organization, but there did not appear to be any.

"Wait, what's this?" said Violet. She pulled a small piece of paper from the top of one of the stacks. The children gathered around to look at the scribbled note:

- ~~Schedule cuckoo clock appraisal~~
- Meeting in park at 7:30—wrap and bring package!
- Send letter to G. H.
- Pick up air cleaner from hardware store

"Look," said Jessie. "It's dated a week ago. That was around the same time that Mr. Muldaur got hurt."

"That's probably why only the first thing on the list got crossed off," said Henry. "Mr. Muldaur never got a chance to do the other things."

"There's something else," said Violet. "Can you read the writing at the top of the list?" The children peered at some very small words on the note. The words seemed to have been written very quickly.

"It looks like a website address," said Jessie slowly. "There's a username and password too."

"'Findyourancestors.com,'" Henry read. "We'd better save this note. It could be important." He pinned it onto the bulletin board on the office wall.

"What's an appraisal?" asked Violet, still looking at the note.

"You get an appraisal when you want to sell something that's valuable, like a house or an expensive antique," said Henry. "You ask an expert to tell you what they think it's worth. The expert writes it all down for you. Then you have a fair price you can charge for the item."

"I'll bet there are appraisals mixed in with these papers," said Jessie. "They would be important to keep."

The bell on the front door jingled. Violet, Jessie, and Henry left the office to see who it was. Benny and Mitzy looked out from behind a shelf.

A tall woman dressed all in black stood at the entrance to the shop. She wore large gold earrings that shone against her dark hair and clothes. Before the children could speak, the woman hurried over to the front counter. She looked up at the shelves behind the counter.

Jessie recognized the woman. It was Lydia Sweeting. She had been Jessie's history teacher at school. "Ms. Sweeting!" Jessie called.

The woman swung around to face Jessie and the other children. "Oh! Jessie Alden!" she said, her eyes widening. "You startled me. What...what are you doing here?"

"We're looking for a birthday present," said Jessie. "We stayed to help Mr. Muldaur. I didn't know you liked antiques, Ms. Sweeting."

"Well, um..." Ms. Sweeting fumbled with the large bag she was carrying. "It's nice to see you while you're on summer break, Jessie," she said. She looked around the shop. "Yes...I *do* like antiques. After all, antiques are all about history."

Jessie smiled. "Is there a special kind of antique

that you collect?" she asked. "Maybe we can help you find it."

Violet pointed to Ms. Sweeting's bag. It had an image of a motorcycle with clock faces for wheels. "That's such a cool design!" said Violet. "Do you collect clocks? Or motorcycles?"

"Or motorcycle clocks?" asked Benny.

Ms. Sweeting blinked a few times. "What? Oh. No, not motorcycles. I mean, yes, I do like motorcycles, but not from an antique shop."

"I saw some old cars in the toy section," said Benny. "Come on, Mitzy. Let's go find Ms. Sweeting a motorcycle."

"Please don't bother!" Ms. Sweeting called after Benny. "I've changed my mind. I need to get home now. I'm...expecting a package in the mail today."

Ms. Sweeting hurried to the door. "It was nice to see you, Jessie," she called as she went out.

Henry, Jessie, and Violet started back toward the office. "That was strange," said Jessie. "Ms. Sweeting is not nervous like that in school."

Henry shook his head. "At first I thought she was

looking for something. But then she didn't want to see a single thing," he said. "Why did she come in?"

"Maybe we just surprised her," said Violet.

"Good point," said Jessie. "Maybe we should let the customers browse a little bit more."

The doorbell jingled again.

The children were going to go back to organizing and let the customer browse, but Mitzy ran to the front of the shop, barking. The dog was usually so calm; the Aldens worried she might break something. They followed Mitzy to the front of the shop.

"Achoo!" A loud sneeze came from the young man near the door. He was bent over Mitzy, who jumped up and wagged her tail. The young man sneezed again and blew his nose on a handkerchief. His long brown hair flew into his face. Then he went back to petting Mitzy. "Good old dog!" he told her, rubbing Mitzy's fur.

"Hello," said Henry. "Are you here to look around?"

The man stood up and pulled his hair back. "Oh, hello," he said. "I just stopped in to see how Mr.

Muldaur was doing...after the accident."

"He's not here right now," Jessie told him. "But he's getting better."

"Do you want to leave a message? We'll tell him you came by," said Violet.

"Oh, no. That's okay," said the man. He looked over toward the back of the shop. "I enjoy seeing Mitzy, anyway." The young man blew his nose again and went out.

Henry shook his head. "I guess I don't understand how antique stores work," he said. "Two people have come by today, but no one was really shopping for anything."

"They barely looked at what was for sale," said Violet.

"And another strange thing: Mitzy seems to know that man," said Jessie. "It was almost like they were friends. Mr. Muldaur would never let anyone pet Mitzy before his bump on the head. How could that man and Mitzy have gotten to be friends?"

It was yet another mystery. The antique shop seemed to have a lot of them.

CHAPTER 3

All Jumbled Up

The next time the doorbell jingled, the Aldens were hard at work. They had looked at a lot of papers to figure out what kinds of information was on them.

"I think I know the best way to organize these," said Jessie. "If we—"

"Hello again!" It was Mr. Muldaur. He was carrying several shopping bags. "How are my young shopkeepers doing?"

"We're fine," said Violet. "Except we didn't sell anything."

"Oh, that's all right," said Mr. Muldaur. "We usually get plenty of people who are just browsing." He put down his bags and started pulling out items. "I bought little price tags. Also, sticky labels, file folders, and markers. I thought they might help get things into better order in the office."

"Great," said Henry. "We're just starting to figure out what to do."

Mitzy trotted into the office and put her nose into a bag. "Don't be a snoop, Mitzy," said Benny.

Mr. Muldaur laughed. "Mitzy's nose is telling her about some treats," he said. "Some for her, and some for my human helpers too!" He handed out fancy frosted doughnuts and small cartons of milk to the children. Mitzy got a big dog bone from the pet store.

As everyone munched on their snacks, they talked about how to organize the office.

"I'm glad you brought labels, Mr. Muldaur," said Jessie. "We have a plan that would use them."

"Very good," said Mr. Muldaur as he sat down at his desk. "Let's hear it."

"Well," said Jessie, "you said before that you weren't sure where things are in the shop. Maybe you could put a number on every shelf. Then you could put that same number on the papers that went with the items on that shelf."

"That sounds pretty good!" said Mr. Muldaur. "If I remember correctly, that's like the way libraries are organized. Each book has a special number that tells you where to put it on a shelf. If a customer comes into my shop and asks about an item, I could find its papers easily. If someone wants an item, maybe I could look it up somehow and know where it is. Maybe..." He drifted off in thought.

"I think that's not quite enough," said Violet. "You could use a map of the store, so you know where each shelf is."

"And," said Henry, "wouldn't you also want a list of everything that's on each shelf? Sort of like having a little map inside a big one?"

"Yes!" cried Mr. Muldaur. "You children are wonders. I'll be able to find everything once you have this place organized." He sat back and sighed. "Well, mostly everything."

Mr. Muldaur put his hand to his head, and Mitzy leaned on his leg. Mr. Muldaur gave a small smile. "She knows when I'm feeling sad."

"Don't worry. Your stories will come back," said Henry. "Didn't the doctors say it might take a while? We can help you in the meantime."

"It's not just my memories I'm sad about," said Mr. Muldaur. "I was thinking about the time I spent in the hospital. It was lonely. I thought I would have visitors. But no one came."

"No one?" asked Violet. "Don't you have family, Mr. Muldaur?"

"From what I've figured out, I have quite a big family," said Mr. Muldaur. "I have all kinds of pictures of family members at home. But I'm sad to say, even that part of my memory hasn't come back yet."

"Do you know if anyone from your family lives in the area?" asked Jessie.

Mr. Muldaur scratched his head. "In the hospital the nurses called my sister, Jean, but she did not come to visit. I have a feeling we must not have been very close before the accident." He lowered his head. "I don't think I was a very good person."

"You should not say that," Jessie told Mr. Muldaur. "You've been so nice to us."

"Besides," said Violet, "maybe you can fix things with your sister. She might be happy to be in touch with you again." Violet sat down next to Mitzy. "Before we met our grandfather, we thought he was mean. But he turned out to be the best grandfather ever."

"You know, someone did worry about you when you were sick," said Henry. "A man visited you today. He knew Mitzy, and he asked how you were doing."

"What was his name?" asked Mr. Muldaur.

"He didn't tell us," said Violet. "He had long brown hair. He really likes your dog. Don't you think he's a friend of yours?"

"I really don't know," said Mr. Muldaur. "Someone who knows Mitzy? I can't remember."

"That's okay," said Henry. "You *will* remember. And that man will come back if he's your friend."

"I hope you're right," said Mr. Muldaur.

Mr. Muldaur and the children started organizing. Violet drew up a map of the store with all its shelves, counters, and tables. Jessie worked on a numbering system for matching papers and items.

Benny went to find the toys. He took the box of keys with him.

Henry and Mr. Muldaur decided to start making

the list of items. They began with the most valuable things, the ones behind the counter.

"I can call out what each item is," said Henry. "Mr. Muldaur, will you tell me if you want to give it a different name after that?"

Mr. Muldaur nodded. "I'll write down the name and what shelf it's on. Let's get going."

Henry looked at the bottom shelf, where there was a locked glass case. "I see a big leather book in there," he said. "It looks like it has a lock on it. Why would someone lock up a book?"

Mr. Muldaur unlocked the case with a key. He bent down and pulled out the book. "This isn't an ordinary kind of book," he said. "It's a stamp collection." He opened the top of the stamp collection and studied the inside. "Let's call this 'Nineteenth-Century American Stamp Book' for now. I hope I have papers in the desk for it."

They went through all the items in the glass case one by one. It took a lot of time, and the list was long. Henry decided to bring his laptop next time. That way, he could put the lists into a spreadsheet to keep track of everything.

Mr. Muldaur was locking the case when Benny appeared. "I haven't found the rest of the toys yet. But I will," he said. "Wow! What's that?" He pointed to one of the clocks high up on a shelf behind the counter. "It looks like part of a time machine!"

Mr. Muldaur chuckled. "That is a mantel clock," he said.

Henry climbed up the small ladder and brought the clock down, setting it on the counter. The clock had many gears, wheels, and springs, which were all visible. The face of the clock was gold colored. And if you looked closely, you could see tiny pictures had been etched into its surface. There were also fancy looking painted numbers for telling the time. The whole clock was surrounded by a single piece of curved glass, and all of it was fitted onto a wooden base.

"Why is it called a mantel clock?" asked Benny. He stared and stared at the clock.

"I wonder if you know what a mantel is, Benny," said Mr. Muldaur.

"I know," said Henry. "In the old days, before electricity and things like furnaces, most rooms had fireplaces. Fireplaces had shelves above them called mantels. Right?"

Mr. Muldaur nodded. "This clock is just the right size—and also very special looking. It could easily sit on someone's living room mantel. It might have been right in the center, where a family could admire it."

"Does it work?" asked Benny. "I want to see all the gears move."

"I don't know," said Mr. Muldaur. "I'll have to look more closely." He rubbed his head. "I don't remember if I have papers for it though."

Henry and Mr. Muldaur started searching through the papers in the middle drawer of the desk, but they didn't find anything about a mantel clock.

"This is what I was afraid of," said Mr. Muldaur. "There are probably a lot of things in this shop that have no papers at all. What was I thinking to have become so disorganized?"

"You were probably too busy helping customers," said Violet.

"And playing with all the neat things you have!" said Benny.

Mr. Muldaur shrugged. "I don't know about that," he said. "But I am thankful for your help in getting organized now. I think we've all done a lot of work today. I'm going to lock up for the night."

All Jumbled Up

Mr. Muldaur turned off the lights. He and the Aldens and Mitzy went to the door.

"What's that?" asked Benny, pointing to a note taped to the outside.

Mr. Muldaur took the note off of the door and read it aloud:

> I'm tired of arguing. You promised to bring me the item, but you didn't come to our meeting. You have betrayed the family. If you won't hand over what is mine, I will take matters into my own hands.

Benny's eyes got big. "What does that mean?" he said.

Mr. Muldaur looked stunned. "I...I have no idea," he said.

"It sounds like someone is really upset," said Jessie. "Do you know who could have written such a thing?"

Mr. Muldaur thought for a moment. Then he sighed. "No, I don't remember." He started to put the note in his pocket.

"Wait!" said Violet. "Can I take a picture of the note? Maybe we can help."

Mr. Muldaur gave a weak smile. He held out the note, and Violet took a photo with her camera.

"Will I see you children tomorrow?" he asked.

"We'll have to check with Grandfather," said Henry. "But we should be able to come in the afternoon."

"Thank you," said Mr. Muldaur. "I'm starting to think I have more things to straighten out than just the papers in my office."

A Note Full of Mysteries

After dinner that evening, the children sat in the living room with Grandfather and Watch. Grandfather was reading the newspaper, while the children went over the strange things that had happened during the day. Violet pulled up her photo of the note on Henry's computer so they could all look at it.

"This note is full of mysteries," said Violet. "Someone is fighting with Mr. Muldaur. Or at least, they *were* fighting with him."

Henry stared at the screen. "It says 'You missed our meeting.' That meeting could have happened while Mr. Muldaur was in the hospital. He probably forgot about the whole thing!"

"Wait a minute," Jessie said slowly. "Remember the list we found on Mr. Muldaur's desk? There was something about bringing a package to a meeting. We know he didn't do all the things on the list. What if the meeting he missed was the one this note is about?"

Violet nodded. "I'll bet it was the same one!" she said. "That would explain why the person is mad about not getting whatever he was going to bring."

"What do you think he was going to bring?" said Benny. "Maybe it was one of those super valuable antiques. That's why they're fighting over it. It's worth a lot of money."

Grandfather looked up from his reading. He knew how good his grandchildren were at solving mysteries. Usually he didn't get involved. But something about their conversation had caught his ear. "Oh, I wouldn't be so sure, Benny. People fight over all kinds of silly things." Grandfather waved the newspaper he had been reading in the air. "Just today, I read about a man who cut down his neighbor's apple tree. When they asked the man why he did it, he said his neighbor had been mowing the grass on his side of the property line for years."

"Really?" said Violet. "That seems like a small thing to be upset about."

"That's the thing about grudges," said Grandfather. "They start small and build up over time. They get much bigger than they need to."

"It's not hard to see why someone might have a grudge against Mr. Muldaur," said Jessie. "He has been hard to get along with in the past."

"But Mr. Muldaur has changed!" said Benny. "He lets us pet Mitzy now."

Jessie smiled at her brother. "He does seem different, but someone is still upset. We need to figure out why."

"I don't understand the part about betraying 'the family,'" said Henry. "What family? Mr. Muldaur's?"

"That's a good question, Henry," Jessie said.

"I think we should look for Mr. Muldaur's family members," said Violet. "Why don't we see if there are other Muldaurs in Greenfield?"

"How do we do that?" said Benny.

"You can look in the white pages," said Grandfather.

"Good idea!" said Henry. He began typing on his computer.

"Why do they call them white pages?" asked Benny. "Aren't all the pages on the computer white?"

Grandfather chuckled. "Believe it or not, Benny, there used to be in a big book that listed almost everyone's name in Greenfield. It was a town directory. The pages of the book were white, so people called it the white pages."

Benny thought about this. "Lots of books have white pages," he said. "I would have called it the big name book."

"We found one!" said Jessie, pointing at the screen.

"'Muldaur, Jean,'" said Henry. "Didn't Mr. Muldaur say his sister was named Jean?"

Grandfather straightened up. "I know Jean Muldaur! She works down at the Blue Plate Diner. I've chatted with her many times."

"Grandfather, you're like the white pages," said

Benny. "You know everybody."

Grandfather laughed. "Not quite, Benny, but I do know a lot of people in Greenfield. How about I introduce you children to Jean Muldaur? I can take you to the diner in the morning. They make excellent breakfasts."

"I'm hungry already," said Benny, "and it isn't even tomorrow."

"Well, then, hurry up and get ready for bed," said Jessie. "It will be tomorrow before you know it!"

***

Early the next morning, Grandfather drove the children to the Blue Plate Diner. On the way, Violet asked, "What if Mr. Muldaur's sister wrote that note? She might be grouchy."

"She isn't that kind of person," said Grandfather. "You'll soon see for yourselves."

The diner was a small cheerful restaurant, decorated in bold colors. The children sat down in a light-blue booth. Grandfather waited till a tall woman in a red waitress uniform came over. She wore round glasses that made her eyes look big.

"Hello, Mr. Alden!" said the waitress. "I haven't

seen you in some time. Are you having breakfast today?"

"Hello to you!" said Grandfather. "I'm not eating here today, but my grandchildren are. I will leave them in your capable hands while I run a few errands."

The waitress smiled and turned to the children. "Hello, children. My name is Jeanie. What can I get you?" She took out a pad and pencil.

Jessie rummaged in her backpack and took out her own notebook and pencil. "You have questions, and so do we," she said. "I hope you have a little extra time for us."

"After we eat," said Benny. "I do my best thinking with food, and I already know what I want."

"Okay," said Jeanie, laughing. "But I think your brother and sisters might need a minute to decide. I'll bring some water and take your orders soon."

"Grandfather was right," whispered Violet after Jeanie had left. "She seems too nice to have written a mean note like the one we found."

The others agreed. "Even if she didn't write the note," said Henry, "we still might learn more about

Mr. Muldaur and his family. Maybe we'll get some clues about the note."

Jeanie came back soon. She took the Alden's orders and promised to return when things quieted down in the restaurant.

It didn't take long for breakfast to appear. "Blueberry pancakes!" said Benny. He bounced in his seat. Then he got busy doing his favorite thing. Before long, he had blueberry juice and whipped cream on his face.

"Benny, you look like an old man with that beard," said Violet. She giggled and took a big bite of her waffles.

Benny smiled and wiped his face with a napkin. "You too, Violet," he said. But Violet's chin was only a little sticky.

Jessie and Henry had eggs and sausages. Everyone drank orange juice.

"I'm glad we found out about this restaurant," said Jessie. "The food is yummy."

Before long, Ms. Muldaur came back. "I have to watch for customers," she said, "but it's quiet for now. What did you want to ask? I can't imagine."

Henry took a swallow of his juice. Then he said, "We've been helping Mr. Muldaur in his shop. We wondered about a few things there."

"Oh!" Ms. Muldaur looked surprised and then a little sad. "You want to know about my brother. I don't know how much I can help. I'm afraid he and I have been out of touch for years." She shook her head. "It got hard to keep trying with him."

"What do you mean?" asked Jessie.

"My brother didn't seem to want to stay in touch," said Ms. Muldaur. She sat down in the booth. "A long time ago, he stopped returning my calls. After a while, I just stopped calling."

"Why do you think he would do that?" asked Violet.

Ms. Muldaur shrugged. "I wish I knew. He was such a nice person when we were younger. At some point, he seemed to have gotten mad at me. I never found out what the problem was."

Ms. Muldaur stood up quickly. She scribbled in her pad. "I've got to go take care of customers now," she said. "Here's your bill. I'm sorry I couldn't be more helpful."

The children thanked Ms. Muldaur and finished their breakfast.

"It seems strange that she doesn't know why he was upset with her," said Violet. "Do you think she was hiding it from us?"

Henry shook his head. "I think she's just busy. Plus, talking about her brother was a sad thing for her. What do you think, Jessie?"

Jessie agreed. "She seems nice to me. I'm going to ask her if she knows anyone in town who might be angry with her brother. Maybe there are other relatives here that he doesn't know about." Jessie got up to pay the bill.

"Jessie!" called Violet. "Can you save me that bill after you pay?"

Jessie nodded and continued up to the register.

"Does Ms. Muldaur know that her brother got hurt?" Benny asked Violet and Henry. "She never asked how he's doing."

"I don't know," said Violet, "but I don't feel right about telling her. That's between her and Mr. Muldaur."

When Jessie came back, she handed Violet a

copy of the bill. "Jeanie says she and her brother are the only children in her family. She doesn't know anyone who would have a problem with him. She also told me that the shop has been in their family for generations."

Benny's eyes got big. "How long is that?"

"Quite a few years," said Jessie. "Think of it this way: Grandfather is two generations from us. If the shop was owned by Mr. Muldaur's great-grandfather, that would be three generations."

"That's a long time," said Benny.

"It is," said Henry. "Remember Grandfather's story about the neighbor with the grudge? Three generations is long enough to make even a small problem into very big deal."

CHAPTER 5

A Scheduled Surprise

After breakfast, Grandfather picked up the children and dropped them off on Main Street outside of Muldaur's Antique Shop. When the children entered the shop, Mr. Muldaur was back in the office.

"I guess we should see if there's anything Mr. Muldaur needs help with," said Henry.

"Wait a moment. There's something I want to check first," said Violet. She pulled out the bill from the diner. "Jessie, can you ask Mr. Muldaur for the angry note we found on the door?"

Jessie went and got the note and set it on the counter next to the bill. Violet bent over the two slips of paper.

"What are you looking for?" asked Henry.

After a minute, Violet said, "I was looking to see if the same person wrote these two notes. That way we can know for sure if Jeanie was the person who wrote the note."

"Good detective work," said Jessie. "What do you think?" She bent over the counter to look alongside her sister.

"I don't really see how the same person could have written these two notes," said Violet. "The note that was on the window has big, swooping letters. Jeanie's handwriting is sharp and simple."

Jessie straightened up. "So Jeanie Muldaur isn't our scary note writer," she said.

"That makes sense," said Henry. "She seemed nice. I think she mostly just wants her brother back."

"Who wants her brother back?" asked Mr. Muldaur, coming out from his office.

The children looked at one another. They hadn't thought about how they would tell Mr. Muldaur about his sister. Finally, Jessie spoke up. "We met your sister, Jean, this morning. We thought she might be the person who wrote the note on the door, but we don't think she is. She's sad about not seeing you."

"This is both wonderful and worrisome news," said Mr. Muldaur. He put down a vase he was carrying. "I'm glad you talked to Jeanie. Did she talk to you about how I treated her? I hardly remember anything—except that something went wrong years ago..."

"She only said you wouldn't return her calls," said Violet. "She's not angry, just sad about it."

A sad look came across Mr. Muldaur's face. "One more thing I need to straighten out," he said. "I don't know where to begin..."

"Let's take it one step at a time," said Henry. "Did you remember anything more today? We're trying to figure out who wrote the note."

Mr. Muldaur shook his head. "I still have no clue. How could I have made someone so upset?"

"Well, we know you missed a meeting when you were in the hospital," said Jessie. "You were supposed to bring a package with you. But you never did that."

Mr. Muldaur thought hard for a moment. "That

must be it. I just hope I find out who it is and why they're so mad."

As Mr. Muldaur was talking, the doorbell jingled. A short woman wearing lots of jewelry came in. She walked right over to Mr. Muldaur and put out her hand to shake. The bracelets on her wrist jangled.

"Hello, Mr. Muldaur! We meet again!" the woman said cheerfully.

"I'm sorry," said Mr. Muldaur. "Do we know each other? I've...had some trouble lately."

"You know me! I'm Sharon Spritz," said the woman. "I do lots of appraisals for you. We have an appointment today." The woman looked around. "Now, what did you want me to appraise today?"

"I—uh...I'm not sure," said Mr. Muldaur. He shifted on his heels and looked around the shop.

Benny spoke up. "Appraisal? I learned that word yesterday. That's when you tell someone how much something is worth, right? Do you find lots of hidden treasures, Ms. Spritz?"

Ms. Spritz smiled. "Very impressive! I guess you could say I do!"

Just then Jessie remembered something. She rushed into the back office and came back holding the to-do list they had pinned to the bulletin board the day before.

"It says here, 'Schedule appraisal for cuckoo clocks.'" Jessie turned to Ms. Spritz. "That must be what Mr. Muldaur wanted you to look at."

"Oh, my favorite!" Ms. Spritz looked around. Her eyes settled on the row of clocks sitting on a shelf behind the main counter. "Those must be the ones." Ms. Spritz opened up her briefcase. She took out a pad of paper, a pen, and a magnifying glass. Quietly, she begin to examine the row of clocks.

Benny had a question he wanted to ask, and he was not good at waiting. He said, "How about that cool one with all the gears? Is that one worth a lot of money?"

Ms. Spritz smiled at Mr. Muldaur. "That's the very clock you asked me about last time I was here! Did you tell this boy to point it out?"

Benny blushed. "No, I just like that one a lot."

"Well, so does Mr. Muldaur," said Ms. Spritz.

Mr. Muldaur tilted his head to the side. "I do?"

he said.

"Of course!" she said. "You told me just last week that this clock had 'personal value' to you. Let's take a look, shall we?"

Henry climbed up the ladder, brought down the mantel clock, and set it on the counter. Ms. Spritz removed the glass cover. She lifted the clock and examined it all over.

"This looks like an heirloom, all right," she said. "It might have been made in the late nineteenth century. One of a kind...handmade..." She carefully turned over the clock and looked at the wooden base through her magnifying glass. "I see a hand-carved maker's mark down here, but it's not one that I recognize from that time period."

"What's a maker's mark?" asked Violet.

"You children ask all kinds of good questions!" said Mrs. Spritz. "A maker's mark is a signature that designers put on objects. Sometimes they're symbols; sometimes they spell out names. You can look up many of them online. I always check for maker's marks on heirlooms like this clock."

"An heirloom!" said Benny. He knew that word

from talking to Mrs. McGregor about her antique collection. "Does that mean it's worth a whole lot of money?"

Ms. Spritz gently set down the clock. "Sometimes," she said. "But in this case, I don't think the clock is worth a lot of money. It was probably made by a local person who wasn't well-known."

A Scheduled Surprise

Ms. Spritz turned to Mr. Muldaur. "And you remember nothing about this clock?"

Mr. Muldaur stared at the clock and sighed. "No," he said. "There *is* something special about it, but I can't say why."

"Well, I really like it too," said Benny. "I want to see how it ticks."

Ms. Spritz laughed. "Maybe you'll get to see just that," she told Benny. "I'll write up an appraisal. Then Mr. Muldaur can see if he can get the clock working. But now, let's take another clock down from that shelf."

Henry helped put other clocks onto the counter. Meanwhile, Jessie, Violet, and Benny talked.

"Mr. Muldaur knows that the clock is special to him," said Violet. "But he doesn't remember *how*. What if the clock is an heirloom from his family?"

Jessie snapped her fingers. "That would explain why Henry and Mr. Muldaur weren't able to find any paperwork for it," she said. "Because it isn't for sale!"

"If the clock is important to Mr. Muldaur's family," said Benny, "does that mean it's what the person who wrote the note is after?"

"I'll bet that's right, Benny," said Jessie.

"But how do we figure out who that person is?" said Violet.

Benny put his fingers up to his chin, thinking. "Maybe we missed someone in the big name book!"

Jessie and Violet laughed.

"It's called the *white pages*, Benny," Jessie said. "And we didn't miss anyone."

But Benny had a good point. If it wasn't another Muldaur, who could it be?

Strange Conversations

After Ms. Spritz had gone, the Aldens got to work organizing. Violet spread out her map of the shop across Mr. Muldaur's desk. Jessie started making labels for the shelves and writing the same numbers into the map. Henry went back to listing items in the shop.

"Come over here, Jessie, Henry. Come, Violet," Benny called. "You should see all the toys!"

Benny had found dozens of antique toys, which had been hidden on shelves behind a big desk. One shelf had delicate dolls with porcelain heads and fancy clothes. Another had mechanical toys. Some had keys in them, but many did not. There were animals, like the bear Benny had found. There were also clowns, farmers, kings and queens, and magicians. Some rode bicycles, and some looked as if they did tricks. There were marionettes and hand puppets, toy trains and cars, and sets of toy soldiers. There was even a wooden farm, complete with a farm family, buildings, and animals.

"I want to know how old these toys are," said Violet. "Then I can picture the boys and girls who might have played with them."

"I want to play with them—all of them!" said Benny. "But I won't. I promise. Hello, Bear." He took the mechanical bear off a shelf and petted it. "We have to get to work so all of these toys can have their keys. Then they can come to life."

Jessie reached to the back of a shelf and pulled out a fancy, red mechanical car. "I'd like to know how these were made," she said, turning the car over and over. "Mr. Muldaur's papers should give us some clues."

"Yes, they should tell us something," said Henry. "And Mr. Muldaur's stories are coming back too! Today, he told me all about the rocking chair and lamp at the front of the shop."

"Hmmm," said Violet. "This is giving me some ideas. I think I have a way for Mr. Muldaur to sell more things." She wandered off down another aisle.

As she did, Mitzy barked a friendly hello and the doorbell jingled. Benny, Jessie, and Henry peered toward the front of the shop to see who it was.

There stood the young man with long brown hair again, scratching Mitzy's head. He looked up—and sneezed.

"Oh, excuse me," he said. "Hi, Mr. Muldaur!" He waved as Mr. Muldaur came out of the office with some boxes. "How are you feeling? It's good to see you back on your feet."

The young man walked along one of the aisles, looking at the shelves. He took a deep breath. "It seems less dusty now," he said. "Did you do something different?"

"I, uh, don't know about that," said Mr. Muldaur. "I'm sorry. I really don't recall." He put down the boxes and went back to his office.

The young man looked confused.

"Mr. Muldaur had a fall last week," Henry explained. "His memory is coming back slowly."

The young man shook his head. "Yes, I heard that he had gotten hurt. But I didn't know it was so bad."

The young man was quiet for a moment. Then he let out a big sneeze, which seemed to snap him out of his thoughts.

"I'm Gary," he said, turning to the Aldens. He noticed the mechanical car Jessie was holding. "Hey, that's the car we were trying to find last spring."

Jessie handed Gary the car, and he admired the old toy. Then he sneezed again.

"Well, I'm glad you found it," the young man told Jessie. He handed back the car. "Put it in a place where Mr. Muldaur can find it easily next time, okay?"

Jessie nodded.

Gary blew his nose. "Well, I've got to run now. Nice to see you all again." He left the shop.

Jessie looked at the others. "That was a little weird, wasn't it?" she said. "It's the second time he has been here. He still wasn't looking for something to buy. So why *was* he here?"

The Mystery of the Forgotten Family

"It does seem strange," said Henry. "I wonder. Is it possible Gary could be the missing family member? The one who wrote the note?"

"He could be," said Violet. "He sure knows Mr. Muldaur. He didn't seem very angry though."

"He knows Mitzy," said Benny. "He knows about things in the shop."

"Too bad we don't know Gary's last name," said Jessie. "If we did, we could call him and ask him some more questions."

As the Aldens got back to work, a few customers came to the shop. One woman who came in with two small children bought a desk lamp. Another woman looked at the jewelry. She finally bought an old ring with a red stone in it. As Violet watched the customers, she kept thinking and thinking. Things were easier to find now, but there was still something missing.

Meanwhile, Benny had a very special job to do. He took all the wind-up toys off the shelf and placed them on a table. Next, he got the box of keys. He tried each key on the toys until he found a match. Then he wound up the toy to see if it worked.

Benny found keys for every toy that didn't have one. The cars raced along, some in straight lines and some in circles. The animals walked or hopped or squawked and stood on their hind legs. The clowns turned somersaults. The kings and queens strutted around and bowed. The farmers raised their pitchforks or dug with hoes. The magicians laughed and spun around.

It had been a good morning. The shop was finally starting to become more lively. At lunchtime, the children took a well-earned break. They brought their lunches to the park, and Mitzy came along for a walk. On the way, Mitzy suddenly stopped and started to growl. A woman was coming toward them on the path.

"Look!" said Benny. "It's that teacher you know, Jessie."

It was Lydia Sweeting, Jessie's history teacher. Jessie waved. "Hi, Ms. Sweeting!"

The woman looked up. "Oh! Hello, Jessie," she said. "I didn't know you all lived around here."

"We don't," said Jessie. "We're still helping out in the antique shop."

Mitzy growled right at Ms. Sweeting.

"Don't do that, Mitzy," Benny told the dog, holding tight to her leash. "That's rude."

"Oh, yes, the antique shop," said Ms. Sweeting. "How is the shop? Are you enjoying yourselves?"

"It's fun," said Benny. "But why were *you* there the other day, Ms. Sweeting? You didn't buy anything."

"Benny!" Jessie put her hand on Benny's shoulder. Sometimes her little brother did not know when *he* was being rude. Even still, she was glad he had asked. Jessie had wondered why Ms. Sweeting had stopped by the shop, and she wanted to hear what the history teacher might say.

For a moment Ms. Sweeting said nothing at all. She just looked startled. "You know," she said finally, "I work in a jewelry and watch repair shop in the summer. I came to the antique shop hoping to find some old watches. Sometimes we take them apart and use their parts to fix other watches. Maybe I'll come back again. When I have more time."

Mitzy barked, and Ms. Sweeting took a step

away. "Well, it was nice seeing you, Jessie. Have a good afternoon, children." Ms. Sweeting steered wide of Mitzy and hurried down the path.

"What's with Mitzy?" asked Violet. "I thought she liked everybody."

"*Almost* everybody," said Jessie, looking down the path after Ms. Sweeting.

The Aldens settled onto a park bench to eat their sandwiches. Henry spoke up. "We need to find out more about that mantel clock. I just know that it's important in this whole thing."

"Ms. Spritz said we could see makers' marks on the internet," said Violet. "We should take the clock home and study it."

"Good idea, Violet," said Henry. "Let's ask Mr. Muldaur if we can do that." He fed Mitzy a corner of his sandwich. "I'm thinking about that clock too. If the clock has been in the family for generations, and it's what the person is upset about, maybe the person we're looking for isn't a brother or sister."

"Good point, Henry. It could be a more distant relative," said Jessie. "We need to learn more about

Mr. Muldaur's *whole* family."

Just as the children finished eating, it began to sprinkle. Together, the Aldens ran with Mitzy back to the shop.

CHAPTER 7

A Timely Clue

Mr. Muldaur gave the Aldens permission to take the clock home. Henry called Grandfather. Because it was raining, he wanted to make sure Grandfather could pick them up right at closing time.

"We'll need to wrap this clock very well and carry it home carefully," Henry said. "I wouldn't want it to get wet."

The children worked with Mr. Muldaur for the rest of the afternoon. They got a lot of organizing done, but there weren't as many customers as there had been when the sun was shining.

Back at home, the Aldens unwrapped the clock. They all sat around a table with the clock in front of them. Mr. Muldaur had gotten it working that afternoon. The children watched as the many wheels, springs, hands, and gears moved smoothly along, telling the time.

"It's amazing that something made so long ago could work this well," said Jessie.

"It was probably well taken care of for most those years," said Henry. "And it was probably well made in the first place."

Violet peered at the clock face. "Those etchings are beautiful," she said. Violet had learned about etchings in her art class. Seeing them up close, she was amazed at the tiny details. Some showed pictures of animals. One was of a sun, and another showed a moon. There were also tiny pictures of a wooden house, a shop on a street, and a horse and carriage.

"These etchings might have clues for us," said Jessie. "We could magnify them to see details. We could try to find similar etchings somewhere."

"Good idea," said Jessie. "Do you remember what Ms. Spritz said? That the clock was made locally? We could go to the library to do research. I know there's a lot of local history we can find there."

A Timely Clue

"Let's ask Grandfather to take us tonight!" said Benny. He didn't like being stuck inside the house when it was raining, and he loved visiting the library.

"Good idea, Benny," said Violet. "First, I'll take some photos of the clock. Then we won't have to bring it along."

That evening, Grandfather drove them to the local library through the rain. Inside, the children worked at the computer. Violet magnified her photos of the clock on the screen. The children could clearly see the maker's mark on the bottom of the clock now. There were initials, *M. M.*, and a curly design underneath the letters.

"I hope we can find this maker's mark on the internet," said Violet. "But let's look at the etchings now." She moved on to a picture that showed a store with a horse and carriage outside.

"Hey!" said Benny. "Are those tiny words across the top of the shop? I can read them, I bet. Can you make the picture even bigger, Violet?"

Violet worked at it. Then she frowned. "The letters just get blurry when I make them bigger," she said. "Can you read them the way they are, Benny?"

Benny tried. "I think...there are two big *M*'s on a sign. Then it says...'Time' and something too small to read." He jumped up. "Maybe it's an antique shop, like Mr. Muldaur's!"

"Maybe," said Jessie. "Or maybe, those two big *M*'s have something to do with the maker's mark."

"So we could be looking at a tiny picture of the shop where this clock was made," said Henry. "I wish I had eagle eyes like yours, Benny. Who knows what else I could find in the world?"

Benny grinned. "These are *my* eyes," he said. "They're people eyes, not eagle eyes."

The Aldens all laughed—even Benny.

Next, the children went online to look for the maker's mark. The internet had some famous marks for clockmakers, but nothing about lesser-known ones. Henry asked for help from the librarian, Mr. Stockwell. The man brought the Aldens over to the part of the library that had local history materials.

"Here you'll find newspapers, books, and other files," said Mr. Stockwell. "Most of this information

isn't online. One day we hope to organize it all and upload it though."

"That would be a great project for another rainy day," said Jessie. "But now we're looking for information about clockmakers from a long time ago."

Mr. Stockwell polished his glasses. "Hmm..." he said. "What year do you think these clockmakers might have been in operation? The town of Greenfield has been around for quite a long time."

Violet thought about the etchings on the clock face. "We think it was before the twentieth century," she said. "Maybe from the days of horses and carriages. Wasn't that before nineteen hundred?"

"Very good," said Mr. Stockwell. "There were horses and carriages in the early nineteen hundreds. Soon, though, most were replaced by cars and other motor vehicles."

"Like tractors and motorcycles?" asked Benny.

"Exactly," said Mr. Stockwell. "Let me know if you children need more help finding things. Right now, I need to head back to my desk."

The Aldens thanked the librarian and turned to

the stacks of books and newspapers.

"Well," said Henry, "what do we know about this clock so far? That will help us decide where to start looking."

"It might have been made in the eighteen hundreds," said Violet. "That's the nineteenth century."

"We found it in Mr. Muldaur's shop," said Jessie. "And people in his family might still be fighting over it."

"What if we look for the name Muldaur along with anything about clocks?" said Henry. "We don't have to go all the way back to the nineteenth century. We can start with our century, the twenty-first, and go backward."

So Jessie and Benny looked in books. Violet and Henry checked newspapers. Some of the books had indexes in the back. Luckily, there were also indexes to the newspapers. That way, the children could look for subjects and find the location of articles and chapters.

"Let's make a list of the subjects we want to find in the indexes," said Jessie. She took out her notebook to write down the list of words.

"How about 'Muldaur'?" said Violet. "Also, 'clockmaker' and 'antique store'?"

Jessie wrote down the list of words, and everyone got to work.

It didn't take long before Benny got antsy. He got up and ran around the table with his arms spread out like a bird's.

"What are you doing, Benny?" Henry asked.

"I'm trying to look with eagle eyes," he said. "But it's a lot harder this way."

The children all laughed.

After a few more minutes of searching, Jessie looked up. "I found something about Muldaur's shop!" she said. "And there's a photo from 1897."

Violet came over to see the photo. "That looks a little bit like Mr. Muldaur's antique shop," she said.

"It looks even more like the picture on the clock face," said Benny. "See? There's the sign above the shop!" Benny pointed excitedly to the photo and read: "'Muldaur's Time Pieces.' And there are the two big *M*'s with the swirly shape underneath them."

A Timely Clue

"Just like the etching!" said Violet. "This is a great clue."

The next thing that happened gave the Aldens more clues.

Henry called Jessie and Benny over. "Listen to this!" he said. "We found an article in an old newspaper. It's about the Muldaur family shop."

The others gathered around Henry as he read aloud. "'In the early days of Greenfield, the name Muldaur meant fine clocks and watches. The Muldaurs had a shop on Main Street. They collected clocks. They also repaired timepieces for many years. One of the Muldaurs—Melissa—designed and made her own clocks for the family.'"

"Hey," said Violet. "That must be whose initials are on the bottom of our clock: Melissa Muldaur!"

"Hooray!" said Benny. "Is that the person we're looking for?"

Jessie grinned. "I don't think Melissa is alive today, Benny. Remember, the clock was passed down from one generation to another."

"That's right," said Henry, "but listen to the rest of the story."

The Mystery of the Forgotten Family

Henry read the newspaper story aloud. It told all about the Muldaur shop. It explained that in the 1920s, two children had inherited the shop. The son, Aaron Muldaur, wanted to turn it into an antique shop. The daughter, Melissa Muldaur, wanted to stick to clock design and repair. For a few years, the shop did both things. But Aaron and Melissa could never agree. They fought over what the shop should be selling. Finally, Melissa left, and Aaron kept it as an antique shop. Melissa started her own business, one that only made and fixed watches and clocks.

"And that's why it is now Muldaur's Antique Shop," said Benny. "Not Muldaur's Time Pieces."

"I think that's also how the whole fight started," said Violet.

"What do you mean?" said Benny.

"I see what you're saying, Violet," Henry said. "The fight that started it all was about more than just a clock. It was about what kind of shop the family should have and who would get to keep the shop. That was all very important to the brother and sister, Aaron and Melissa. I can see why the argument might have lasted for years and years."

"But we still don't know who is threatening Mr. Muldaur today," said Jessie.

"It's got to be someone in Mr. Muldaur's family," said Henry.

"Wouldn't Mr. Muldaur have known that person?" asked Benny. "We know who is in *our* family."

Jessie said, "Mr. Muldaur might have never known. It could be a second or third cousin. It's probably someone from Melissa Muldaur's side. After all, they were the ones who didn't keep the shop."

The Aldens put away the books and newspapers.

"We learned a lot tonight," said Violet. "Maybe Mr. Muldaur can help us with the rest in the morning."

But the morning brought new surprises.

Break-In, Breakthrough

When the children arrived at Muldaur's Antique Shop, Mr. Muldaur was outside. He stood on the sidewalk, staring at the door and scratching his head.

"What's wrong?" asked Violet. She was holding the mantel clock they had brought home. "Was there another accident?"

"I don't think this was an accident," said Mr. Muldaur. "Someone broke into the shop last night."

The children looked at the storefront. Nothing looked to be wrong. "How did they get in?" said Jessie. She was sure Mr. Muldaur had locked up the day before.

"I'm not sure," said Mr. Muldaur. "There's no

broken glass or anything like that. But the door was open when I got here."

"Is anything missing?" asked Henry.

Mr. Muldaur shook his head. "I'm not sure yet. But..."

"Look!" said Benny, pointing to the ground. There were small screws and a bolt lying just inside the doorway. Benny knelt down and picked up something shiny and smooth.

"That's the doorknob," said Mr. Muldaur. "Whoever broke in knew how to take the lock apart. Who could do that?"

"Let's go inside," said Jessie. "We will help you find out what the person took."

"I'll have a look at the safe and the cash register," said Mr. Muldaur. "A robber would try to get into those, I bet."

"And I'll see if I can put that lock back together," said Henry. "I just need the toolbox from the office."

Inside the shop, some items had been taken down from their shelves, and some of the furniture was moved, but nothing appeared to be broken.

In the office, papers were scattered over the floor. The file cabinet drawers were pulled out.

"Someone was definitely looking for something in particular," said Jessie. "Let's get these papers back in order. Then we'll know if anything is missing from the office."

After a little while, Mr. Muldaur came into the office. "The money is all here," he said. "None of the jewelry is gone either. In fact, I can't think of anything that's missing!"

Despite the mess, the Aldens could not find anything missing in the office either.

"Why would someone break in and not take anything?" asked Jessie, closing up one of the file cabinets.

"Maybe they were looking for something that wasn't here!" said Benny. "Because we had it at home!"

"The clock!" said Mr. Muldaur. "Do you think that is what they were after? Does this have something to do with that note?"

The children told Mr. Muldaur what they had learned about the clock and the history of the shop.

Mr. Muldaur shook his head. "It all makes sense. Now, if I could only remember who that person was," he said. He took a deep breath. "Well, until then, let's clean up."

The Aldens got to work putting the shop back in order. The doorbell jingled several times as customers came to browse and to buy. Then a familiar sneeze came from the doorway, and Mitzy bounded forward. The young man, Gary, stood in the doorway petting the dog.

"Again?" said Violet to her sister quietly. "He keeps coming here."

Jessie put down the vase she was carrying and went to the front of the shop.

"Hello there," she said to Gary. "What brings you in today?"

Gary blew his nose and looked up. He smiled. "Oh, just the usual," he said. "I'm saying hello to my favorite dog." He looked around. "It's a little different here. Are you rearranging?"

"Someone rearranged while the shop was closed last night," said Jessie. "There was a break-in." Jessie watched Gary carefully.

"Uh-oh," said Gary. He stopped petting Mitzy. "Was anything taken? Any damage?" He looked worried.

"We don't think so," said Jessie. "That's what is so strange. Do you know anyone who would want to break in and take something?"

Gary shook his head. "I sure don't," he said. "Mr. Muldaur doesn't have many friends, but I didn't think he had enemies either. There's never been a robbery here. I would know if there had been."

With that, the young man followed Mitzy down one of the aisles. Jessie thought he might buy something, so she went back to cleaning up.

But Violet had other ideas. She had moved several tables to the middle of the shop, where they stood together. Then Violet had arranged ceramic figurines on each table. One table had animals and people that were painted in pale colors. Another table had figurines that were all in black and white. The middle table had brightly painted figurines. Most of those were painted in shades of purple, from grape to magenta to deep violet.

"What do you think?" Violet asked Jessie. "Don't

these ceramics look good together? Wouldn't you want to buy them now that I've set them this way?"

Jessie smiled. "It's beautiful, Violet," she said. "You have a wonderful eye. I'm sure this will help Mr. Muldaur sell more of these antiques."

When things had been put back in the front of the shop, the girls returned to the office. Henry had stacked most of the loose papers into neat piles on the desk and was sorting through them.

Benny was under the desk. "Hey, what is this?" he said. He crawled backward from under the desk and held up an envelope.

"Whew," he said. "It's dusty under there! I wonder how long this has been hiding." Benny wiped some dust off the envelope and gave it to Henry.

"This has the name Gary Hughes on it," said Henry. "It's not sealed. Let's see what's inside." Henry pulled out two pieces of paper. "This one is a check," said Henry. "The other one is a letter."

Henry sat down and read the letter. "It says that Mr. Hughes's last paycheck is in the envelope. The letter is from Mr. Muldaur. He says he's sorry that he wasn't a better boss. He wishes that he had cleared up the problem with the dust mites. Then Mr. Hughes might not have quit working for him."

"Dust mites?" said Benny. "What are those?"

Henry said, "They're tiny creatures that live in dust. People can be really allergic to dust mites."

Benny looked at his dusty hands. "I've never seen anything crawling in dust," said Benny. "They must be invisible."

"No, Benny," said Henry. "Dust mites are microscopic. That means you need a microscope to see them because they're so small."

"Hold on," said Jessie. "Did you say the person's name was Gary Hughes?"

"Hey, we know someone named Gary," said Violet.

"A Gary who sneezes a lot!" said Benny.

CHAPTER 9

A Test and a Tree

"Mr. Muldaur!" The children rushed out of the office to the front counter, where the shopkeeper was working.

"Is everything okay?" Mr. Muldaur asked.

The children showed him the check and the letter he'd written. For a moment, he did not understand. Then a sad look appeared on his face as he finished reading the letter. He sighed. "I never gave Gary the check or the letter. He must be furious with me."

"Do you remember Gary now?" asked Violet.

Mr. Muldaur scratched his head where his bandage had been. "Yes, it's coming back to me now. Gary worked in the shop for years. We were friends. But he had to quit about a month ago. His allergies had gotten too bad for him to stay."

"Gary stopped in a few times," said Violet. "He asked about you every time."

"In fact," said Jessie, "he might still be here! Mitzy, where did Gary go?" Mitzy just wagged her tail and turned toward the back of the shop.

A sneeze came from the direction of the office.

"I think I know the answer to that question!" said Benny. Henry stayed to help the other customers in the shop. Everyone else rushed to the office.

They found Gary sifting through papers on the desk. He looked up suddenly and dropped the papers he was holding. "Oh! Whoops!" he said. "I was just trying to find..."

"Your paycheck?" asked Mr. Muldaur. He held up the check and the letter.

"I'm really sorry," said Gary. "I got tired of coming over and not being able to get my paycheck. And with you not remembering, Mr. Muldaur...I thought I'd look for the check myself. I didn't mean to snoop around."

"It's all right, Gary. I understand," said Mr. Muldaur. "I should have given you your check

some time ago. I should have cleaned up this place so you could stay and work here too."

Mr. Muldaur sat down at the desk. Then he continued, "Now that my memory is coming back, I can see how I treated you. I wish I had done something about your allergies. I guess I was a pretty bad friend."

"But, Mr. Muldaur, you *were* planning to do something," said Jessie. She pulled the to-do list off the bulletin board. "See? It says, 'Pick up air cleaner from hardware store.' You had your accident before you could run that errand."

Mr. Muldaur gave a small smile. "Still, it seems as if I closed the barn door after letting out the horses."

Benny was confused. "Where are your horses now, Mr. Muldaur?" he asked. "We can help you find them!"

"Oh, Benny," said Mr. Muldaur, smiling. "That's just an expression."

"He means that he did try to take care of the problem," said Jessie. "He just waited until *after* Gary quit his job."

"I'm really sorry I don't work here anymore," said Gary. "Mr. Muldaur, you and I really did well together. Do you remember?"

Mr. Muldaur nodded.

Gary went on. "The only problem for me was my allergies. If you could fix that problem, I'd be happy to come back to work."

Mr. Muldaur handed Gary his check. "I intend to make this shop much less dusty," he told Gary. "And more organized! I hope you can come back soon."

Gary promised to stay in touch. Then he left the shop.

"It's time for me to go take care of customers," said Mr. Muldaur. "I'll send Henry back here. You children can take a break and have a snack."

Henry, Violet, and Benny shared some fruit and homemade cookies Mrs. McGregor had packed for them. But Jessie didn't stop to eat. She kept looking at Mr. Muldaur's to-do list.

"I think this list is starting to make sense now," she said. "Look." She showed the piece of paper to the others.

A Test and a Tree

- ~~Schedule cuckoo clock appraisal~~
- Meeting in park at 7:30—wrap and bring package!
- Send letter to G. H.
- Pick up air cleaner from hardware store

"I see what you mean," said Henry, munching a berry. "Mr. Muldaur scheduled the appraisal with Ms. Spritz. We were in the shop when that happened."

"G. H. stands for Gary Hughes," said Violet. "That explains the letter we found in Mr. Muldaur's office. And..."

"'Pick up air cleaner' means that Mr. Muldaur was going to get rid of the dust mites," said Benny. "So Gary wouldn't sneeze so much."

"Right," said Jessie. "We also know something about that meeting in the park that never happened."

"It was about the clock," said Benny.

"But we still don't know who Mr. Muldaur was going to meet," Violet added.

"I don't think it could have been Gary," said Jessie. "What do you think, Henry?"

Henry shook his head. "Gary wasn't interested in getting a package from Mr. Muldaur," he said. "He just wanted his paycheck. And his old job."

Jessie nodded. "Now we need to find out who Mr. Muldaur was going to meet," she said. "That's the person who's angry with him."

"Well, we know a few things about that person," said Violet. "We know they probably broke into the shop."

"They're really smart about taking things like doorknobs apart," said Benny.

"They are probably related to Mr. Muldaur too," said Henry.

The children stood in silence for a moment, unsure of what to do next. Then Violet spoke up. She was holding the to-do list in her hand. "There's one more thing on this paper. It talks about 'ancestors.'" She pointed to the writing above the list. "Could it be a clue?"

Henry, Jessie, and Benny gathered around. They had been so focused on the items on the list, they had forgotten all about the website and login information scribbled at the top.

A Test and a Tree

"Good thinking, Violet," said Jessie. "Mr. Muldaur must have visited that address before the accident. Let's see what it is."

The children used Mr. Muldaur's computer in the office. They discovered that Find Your Ancestors was a website that helped people find their relatives.

"This company asks you to take a DNA test," said Jessie. "You send in your test, and they can find people you're related to."

"How do you take a DNA test?" asked Benny. "Is it like a spelling test?"

"This is a much different kind of test, Benny," said Henry. "I learned about it in science class. You have to send a small amount of your saliva to the company."

"It's a spit test?" said Benny. "Gross!"

Henry shook his head. "Your DNA is in your saliva," he explained. "DNA is like an invisible code that tells a lot about you. It can tell who you are, where you come from, and who might be in your family."

"All that just from a little saliva," said Violet. "And you can see your whole family tree!"

Benny was still confused. "A tree?" he asked. "What does a tree have to do with a family? Is that another one of those expressions?"

"That's exactly what it is, Benny," said Violet. "A family tree is just a chart of the people in your family."

Jessie entered the username and password from the to-do list. A chart came up on the screen. The children studied it.

"This is definitely Mr. Muldaur's chart," said Henry.

"I see his name," said Benny.

"I see Jeanie Muldaur's name too," said Violet. "It's right there, under 'sister or brother'!"

Jessie said, "Let's follow this chart back a few generations. Remember that Muldaur's Antique Shop was in the family. But then a brother took over and a sister decided to go into business for herself."

"Look!" said Benny. "There's Melissa Muldaur, right next to her brother, Aaron."

The Aldens followed the chart down Melissa Muldaur's family tree, hoping to find a name they might recognize. But when they came to a name they all knew, it was not a Muldaur at all.

"Lydia Sweeting!" said Henry.

"My history teacher?" said Jessie.

"And Mr. Muldaur's second cousin!" said Violet.

CHAPTER 10

Family Reunion

The children excused themselves from the shop. With the new information, they needed to see someone right away.

"Ms. Sweeting said she works in a watch repair shop in the summer," said Jessie.

"There's only one of those in Greenfield," said Henry. "Let's go there."

Right down Main Street went the Aldens. Just as they got to the watch repair shop, they saw Ms. Sweeting. She had just stepped outside and was holding her big black bag, the one with the motorcycle with clocks for wheels. She looked up and seemed startled to see the children.

"Hi, Ms. Sweeting," said Jessie. "We came to talk

to you. Do you have some free time?"

"Um, yes, I suppose so," said Ms. Sweeting. "I was leaving work for the day. What is it you children need?"

"We want to talk to you about a clock," said Jessie. "A particular clock in Mr. Muldaur's shop."

"Oh my," Ms. Sweeting sighed. She looked up and down the street. "Can we go somewhere more private and sit down to talk?"

"How about the park?" said Violet. "It's right nearby." Ms. Sweeting agreed.

When they were all seated on park benches, Henry began. "Did you know that you and Mr. Muldaur are in the same family?"

"Yes, I did know that," said Ms. Sweeting. "He and I are distantly related. Our family tree goes back a pretty long way."

"We saw your tree," said Benny. "We saw it on a computer. And we read a story about an old family argument."

"Oh!" Ms. Sweeting blinked a few times. She fumbled with one of her earrings. Then she folded and unfolded her hands.

"We're wondering if that old argument is still going on," said Jessie.

"And we're wondering if you are the person who left a note on the shop door," said Violet. "We think it might have something to do with a break-in at the shop."

Ms. Sweeting gave a big sigh. "You always were sharp, Jessie," she said. "I should have known you children would figure it out. I might as well tell you the rest."

Ms. Sweeting shook her head. Her dangling earrings made little tinkling sounds. "A couple of years ago, I did some research into my family," she said. "I learned that I come from a long line of people interested in clock making. That didn't surprise me. I love to tinker with clocks and watches. I also found the connection between Mr. Muldaur and myself. So the next time I went to his shop, I looked around for anything that might belong to our family. When I saw the mantel clock he had, I took a good long look at it. That was when I realized that it had been made by my great-grandmother, Melissa Muldaur, who became

Melissa Sweeting by marriage."

Ms. Sweeting sat up straight on the bench. "That was also the moment our argument began."

"You thought the clock belonged to your side of the family, not Mr. Muldaur's, right?" asked Jessie.

"Yes," said Ms. Sweeting. "I thought he should give me the clock, but he wouldn't. He said it belonged to the Muldaurs, not to the Sweetings. Oh, we had many an argument over the months! It took such a long time, but finally he gave in. He told me he would let me have the clock."

Ms. Sweeting looked back toward Main Street and the antique shop. "I remember that day. His dog kept barking at me. When we finally stopped arguing, the dog sat down, quiet as a mouse."

Benny nodded. "Mitzy wouldn't like people fighting with her owner. That must be why she growled at you when we passed you in the park."

"I'm sure it was," Ms. Sweeting said.

"But Mr. Muldaur never gave you the clock," said Violet.

"That's right," said Ms. Sweeting. "He had agreed to meet me. I waited and waited in the park that evening...but he never came. I lost patience after that."

"Did you know that he got hurt and was in the hospital?" asked Henry. "He was planning to meet you. But he couldn't be there."

"No, I had no idea," said Ms. Sweeting. She looked surprised by the news. "But why didn't he try to reach me when he felt better?"

"He bumped his head and couldn't remember things," said Benny.

Ms. Sweeting looked out over the park, taking the information in. "And all this time, I thought he had betrayed the family. It's a bad feeling when someone promises to do a thing and they never do it."

"You got really angry with him after that, didn't you?" asked Violet.

Ms. Sweeting nodded. "But if what you children are saying is true," she said, "I wish I hadn't gotten so angry. I didn't know Mr. Muldaur was sick. I only made things worse. I'm sorry for all of that."

Henry shifted on his seat. "I've been wondering something. That time we first saw you at the shop, were you looking for the clock?"

"Yes," said Ms. Sweeting. "I waited till Mr. Muldaur left, then I went in. I thought no one would be there. But you children surprised me."

"And the night of the break-in," said Violet, "it was you who took apart the lock, wasn't it?"

"That's right," said Ms. Sweeting. "I looked everywhere for that clock but couldn't find it."

"That's because it was at our house that night!" said Benny.

"So *that's* where it was! I thought for sure I had just missed it," said Ms. Sweeting. She stood up. "You know, I think it's time I speak with Mr. Muldaur. I want to get everything out in the open. What do you children think?"

"Agreed!" said the children at once.

Ms. Sweeting shook hands with each of the Aldens. Then everyone headed to the antique shop.

Mr. Muldaur was just coming out from the back of the shop. He was carrying a stack of boxes. Mitzy started to bark when she saw Ms. Sweeting.

Benny hurried over. "It's okay, Mitzy," he said, hugging her. "No one's going to argue anymore."

The children and Ms. Sweeting explained the

whole story to Mr. Muldaur, and Ms. Sweeting apologized for leaving the note and breaking into the shop.

Mr. Muldaur listened closely, but he did not look upset. When Ms. Sweeting was done, Mr. Muldaur sighed. "Thank you for your apology. But I think it is I who should apologize to *you*. I'm sorry you had to keep fighting to get what was yours all along. What a bothersome person I've been! I guess that bump on the head was good for me. Otherwise, I would still be holding on to some old grudges."

"But, Mr. Muldaur," said Jessie, "you were already changing before your accident."

"That's right," said Violet. "Before your fall, you had planned to give the clock to Ms. Sweeting. You knew it belonged to her from your ancestor test."

"That might have been how you fell off the ladder," said Henry. "You were climbing up to get the clock!"

"I suppose that's all true," said Mr. Muldaur. "I don't like the idea of burning bridges though." He turned to Ms. Sweeting. "Will you come back as a customer some time?"

Ms. Sweeting smiled. "Of course," she said. "I'm always looking for watch and clock parts."

Henry brought down the mantel clock one last time. He gave it to Mr. Muldaur, who handed it to Ms. Sweeting.

"I think this old family feud has finally ended," Mr. Muldaur told Ms. Sweeting. "We have these children to thank for it."

"I believe you're right," said Ms. Sweeting. She put the clock carefully into her bag. "Good-bye for now, Mr. Muldaur," she said. "Good-bye, children." Then she left the shop.

"Speaking of burning bridges," said Mr. Muldaur, "I have something else to do."

"Should we call the fire department?" asked Benny.

Mr. Muldaur laughed. "Benny, this time I think you know."

"What do you think I know?" asked Benny.

"That I'm just using an expression," said Mr. Muldaur.

"Burned a bridge," said Jessie, "means you broke something that you can't fix later."

"Okay," said Benny. "What bridge did you burn, Mr. Muldaur?"

"The one I had with my sister, Jeanie," Mr. Muldaur said. "I'm going to see her. I'll find out if that bridge is still standing."

"If it isn't," said Henry, "I'll bet you can build a new one."

Mr. Muldaur laughed again. "You children make me feel as though I can do almost anything! Thank you for helping out in all the ways you have this week."

"You're welcome," said Jessie. "We enjoyed it."

Mr. Muldaur turned to the counter to get a shopping bag. "Now, I have that salt server all wrapped up and ready to go," he said. "By the way, while you children were out just now, I discovered a beautiful new display in the center of the shop. Do you know that I've already sold three items from that display?"

Violet smiled wide. "I thought it might help," she said.

"You'll find one more gift inside this bag," said Mr. Muldaur. "It's just a small thing to remind you all of me."

"We won't forget you, no matter what!" said Benny.

"We'll let you know how Mrs. McGregor likes her antique," said Violet.

"And we'll take Mitzy for some long walks," said Jessie. "Maybe she can meet Watch!"

The Aldens waited till they got home to open the gift bag. First, they took out a beautifully wrapped present for Mrs. McGregor.

And then, in the bottom of the bag was Benny's mechanical bear, with the little key in its side.

Benny grinned. "I know just the spot for this," he said. "I'm going to put it on the mantel—right in the middle!"

**Turn the page to read a
sneak preview of**

MYSTERY AT
CAMP SURVIVAL

**the new
Boxcar Children mystery!**

Six-year-old Benny Alden howled at the TV. He was watching his favorite show, *Wildman Willie*. The man on the show practically lived outdoors, and in each episode, someone hired him to solve a problem.

This week a wolf had been separated from its pack and was trying to hurt a farmer's chickens. The farmer had hired Wildman to take the wolf back to its pack. Wildman had tracked the animal all day. Now it was getting dark outside, but he was too close to give up.

Wildman howled like a wolf, "WhooooOOOOO."

Benny howled like a wolf, "WhooooOOOOO."

Wildman listened.

Benny listened.

In the distance, a wolf howled back. The howl was leading Wildman to the wolf's den.

Suddenly, Wildman stopped. Benny leaned closer to the TV. Wildman poked a stick into what looked like a pile of mushy rocks. "Fresh wolf scat," he whispered. "We're gettin' real close."

Benny's heart raced. He knew from the show that *scat* was another name for animal poop. Old scat turned hard. Mushy scat like this meant the wolf was nearby. Benny barely breathed as Wildman ran through the woods. He would find the wolf. Wildman Willie *always* found what he was looking for.

"Ben-ny. Oh, *Ben*-ny."

Benny didn't hear his sister calling for him. He was tracking the wolf with Wildman.

"Ben-ny. *Ben*-ny. There you are." Ten-year-old Violet stepped in front of the TV. She held a basket of laundry.

"Violet!" cried Benny. He tried to look around her. "Wildman is about to find the wolf!"

"And *we* are about to fold laundry," said Violet. "I'll only move if you promise to help."

Benny nodded and tried to see the TV. Violet sighed and sat down.

"A wolf has been sneaking into a farmer's yard. It's trying to hurt the chickens," said Benny.

Violet shivered. "How awful." The T-shirt she'd been folding lay forgotten in her hands. Sister and brother watched as Wildman eased a rifle off his shoulder. Violet gasped.

"Don't worry," said Benny. "Wildman won't hurt the wolf. That rifle shoots tank...tank..."

"*Tranq*uilizer darts?" she asked.

"Yes," said Benny. "They'll make the wolf sleep so Wildman can take it back to its pack."

Wildman stopped and whispered to the camera, "There's the den. The wolf's inside."

A commercial came on. One always did just before the show's ending.

"Socks," said Violet.

Benny dug through the laundry basket, searching for all the socks. His thoughts drifted back to when he and his brother and sisters had lived in the woods.

After their parents had died, the four Alden children had run away. They'd heard they would be sent to live with a grandfather they'd never met. They thought he would be mean. At first, they had lived outside. Then one night they'd found an old railroad car. The children had turned the boxcar into a cozy home. After a while, their grandfather found them. He'd been searching everywhere for them, and it turned out he wasn't mean at all. Now they all lived together in Grandfather's house.

The commercials ended, and Wildman Willie came back on. He put a finger to his lips, reminding the people watching to stay quiet. Benny and Violet held their breath as Wildman tiptoed toward a mound of leaves. He raised his rifle. They jumped as Wildman yelled, "HUH!" A startled wolf dashed from its den. Wildman pulled the trigger. A tranquilizer dart shot into the wolf's rear end. Slowly, the wolf rolled onto its side, asleep.

"He did it! He did it!" yelled Benny.

Violet clapped her hands. "That was exciting!"

Fourteen-year-old Henry and twelve-year-old Jessie ran in. "What's all the noise?" Jessie asked.

"Wildman Willie caught the wolf," said Benny.

"Judging from all that noise, I think *you're* the Wildman," said Henry, roughing his little brother's hair.

Henry and Jessie sat on the floor and helped sort

laundry. Their dog, Watch, curled up on the sofa. On the TV, Wildman introduced the Show Us Your Adventure part of the show. In it, Wildman showed off photos and videos people had submitted of their own adventures in the wild. Benny really, *really* wished he could be on the show. He looked at the polka-dot sock in his hands. A video of him folding socks wouldn't be very exciting. "I miss living in the boxcar," he said. "It was so much fun."

Jessie tossed him the matching sock. She thought about reminding him that there were hard times in the boxcar too, like the time Violet had gotten sick. The children had been lucky to have help close by when that had happened. Instead, she said, "Wildman is never alone. He has a whole bunch of people along with him. You just don't see them because they are off camera."

Benny shrugged. "He still *does* all the cool stuff himself. Last week he jumped into a frozen lake."

Henry chuckled. "Why would anyone do that?"

"To show people how to get out," said Benny. "I've learned all sorts of survival tricks from Wildman."

On the TV, Show Us Your Adventure ended.

The scene changed to Wildman Willie lifting the sleeping wolf into his rescue plane. "I'm flying this wolf to a new home deep in the wilderness," said Wildman. "There he'll be back with his pack and won't be harming nice people's chickens." Wildman saluted the camera. Benny saluted back. "Until next time," said Wildman. "Be smart. Stay safe." He climbed into his plane and took off into the sky.

The children finished stacking the folded clothes. "Camp Survival!" boomed a voice from the TV. "Where campers survive in the wilderness just like Wildman Willie."

Benny whirled around. "Wha—?"

"Yes," boomed the deep voice, "you too can camp outdoors, forage for food, cook over campfires." The commercial showed happy children toasting marshmallows on sticks over a fire. "Camp Survival. Big Pine Lake, Maine. For children six to sixteen years of age. Register now."

"I'm six!" shouted Benny. "I could go to—"

"Lunch is ready," called a woman's voice. It was Mrs. McGregor, the Aldens' housekeeper.

"Coming!" said Henry, clicking off the TV.

Camp Survival, thought Benny. He had to remember that name. *Camp Survival. Camp Survival*. He just *had* to.

***

Mrs. McGregor bustled around the kitchen, pouring milk and setting out a platter of sandwiches. Mrs. McGregor took care of the Aldens' cooking and cleaning. She was also a close part of the Alden family.

Grandfather walked in. His blue eyes twinkled as he looked at his grandchildren. "Is there room for one more?"

"Here," said Benny, patting the chair next to him.

"Thank you, Benny," said Grandfather. "What are you eating?"

"PB and J," said Benny.

"A fine choice." Grandfather searched the platter for another peanut butter and jelly sandwich.

"There's a..." Benny started. "There's a camp called..." But he had forgotten the name. "It's called..." He closed his eyes and thought of campers fishing and cooking and surviving on their own. "Camp Survival!" he said. "Kids live in the wild just like Wildman Willie. Can we go? Please. Please. *Please?*"

Grandfather chewed thoughtfully. "Where is this camp?"

"Big Pine Lake, Maine," said Jessie.

Something changed in Grandfather's face. "Big Pine Lake, huh?" He took another bite of sandwich. "What do the rest of you think?"

"I'd like to research Camp Survival," said Jessie. She was a whiz at finding out things online. "We'll see if they have interesting programs. If campers like going there. If the counselors are nice."

Grandfather turned to Violet. "What about you?" he asked.

"I would love to sketch life in the woods," she said. "Trees, flowers, animals. Like I did when we lived in the boxcar."

"Hmm," said Grandfather. "Henry?"

Henry speared a pickle from the jar. "I've been studying outdoor survival in Boy Scouts," he said. "It would be fun to try things I've learned."

Grandfather finished his milk. "Jessie," he said,

"why don't you research the camp on the computer. I'll make some phone calls. We'll talk everything over at dinner."

"Hoo-RAY!" yelled Benny.

Grandfather held up a hand. "Hold on," he said. "It's not a yes. It's a 'we'll see.'"

All afternoon, Benny ran back and forth between Jessie's room and Grandfather's office. Jessie printed out information about the camp. They learned that the first two days would be spent learning skills. Then their skills would be put to the test on a three-day hike. Jessie also found online reviews posted by past campers. It seemed like everyone had a good time, except for one girl who got poison ivy. She posted a selfie of her face covered with a rash. "My bad," she said. "I forgot to watch where I was walking."

By dinnertime, it was settled. "Well," said Grandfather, "it looks like the Aldens are on their way to Camp Survival."

***

A week into their summer vacation, the children dragged duffel bags up from the basement. They wrote their names on clothing tags. Jessie was racing past the kitchen with an armload of blankets when she heard Grandfather's hearty laugh. *Is he speaking with Mrs. McGregor?* she wondered.

Jessie peeked into the kitchen. Grandfather was sitting with Watch. "Yes, yes," he was saying into the phone. "He is a fine traveler. You can take him anywhere. He's young and eager—always first on and first off."

Jessie smiled. It sounded like Grandfather was talking about Benny, who always raced to be first—first to the table, first to the door, first to the car. "Oh, yes," said Grandfather. "He'll do just fine up in the air."

Jessie carried the blankets upstairs. "Up in the air?" The Aldens were driving to camp, not flying. What could "up in the air" mean? And who was Grandfather talking to in such a friendly way?

The night before the children left, they gathered in the living room to double-check their packing list. Watch rested his head on his paws. His eyes looked sad. "I'm afraid he knows we're going away," said Jessie. The children liked having

Watch along on their adventures, and Watch loved being outdoors, but Camp Survival did not allow pets.

"Don't worry," said Henry. "Mrs. McGregor will give him extra treats and let him run through the sprinkler."

Violet nuzzled Watch's head. "She does spoil him when we're away."

The next morning, Mrs. McGregor and Watch waited as Henry helped Grandfather lift the duffel bags into the back of the minivan. One by one, each child hugged their sad-eyed dog.

"Time to go," called Grandfather. The children scrambled into the van. As they buckled up, Grandfather walked around to the back. He moved their duffels then closed the door. Soon they were on their way to Camp Survival.

It wasn't until they reached the highway that they found they had a stowaway.

Add to Your
Boxcar Children Collection
with New Books and Sets!

The first sixteen books are now available in
four individual boxed sets!

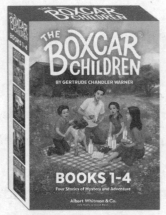

978-0-8075-0854-1 · US $24.99

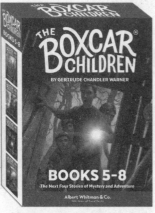

978-0-8075-0857-2 · US $24.99

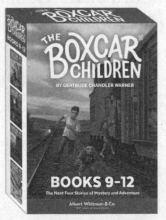

978-0-8075-0840-4 · US $24.99

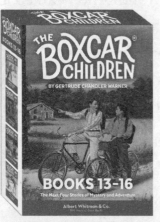

978-0-8075-0834-3 · US $24.99

The Boxcar Children 20-Book Set includes Gertrude
Chandler Warner's original nineteen books,
plus an all-new activity book, stickers,
and a magnifying glass!

978-0-8075-0847-3 · US $132.81

Introducing The Boxcar Children Early Readers!

Adapted from the beloved chapter books, these new early readers allow kids to begin reading with the stories that started it all.

HC 978-0-8075-0839-8 · US $12.99
PB 978-0-8075-0835-0 · US $3.99

HC 978-0-8075-7675-5 · US $12.99
PB 978-0-8075-7679-3 · US $3.99

HC 978-0-8075-9367-7 · US $12.99
PB 978-0-8075-9370-7 · US $3.99

HC 978-0-8075-5402-9 · US $12.99
PB 978-0-8075-5435-7 · US $3.99

HC 978-0-8075-5142-4 · US $12.99
PB 978-0-8075-5139-4 · US $3.99

Check out the Boxcar Children Interactive Mysteries!

Have you ever wanted to help the Aldens crack a case? Now you can with these interactive, choose-your-path-style mysteries!

978-0-8075-2850-1 · US $6.99

978-0-8075-2860-0 · US $6.99

GERTRUDE CHANDLER WARNER discovered when she was teaching that many readers who like an exciting story could find no books that were both easy and fun to read. She decided to try to meet this need, and her first book, *The Boxcar Children,* quickly proved she had succeeded.

Miss Warner drew on her own experiences to write the mystery. As a child she spent hours watching trains go by on the tracks opposite her family home. She often dreamed about what it would be like to set up housekeeping in a caboose or freight car—the situation the Alden children find themselves in.

While the mystery element is central to each of Miss Warner's books, she never thought of them as strictly juvenile mysteries. She liked to stress the Aldens' independence and resourcefulness and their solid New England devotion to using up and making do. The Aldens go about most of their adventures with as little adult supervision as possible—something else that delights young readers.

Miss Warner lived in Putnam, Connecticut, until her death in 1979. During her lifetime, she received hundreds of letters from girls and boys telling her how much they liked her books.